No Bones About It!

Discovering Dinosaurs

by Anna Prokos • illustrated by Gideon Kendall

RED CHAIR ·PRESS·

Imagine That! books are produced and published by Red Chair Press

Red Chair Press LLC   PO Box 333   South Egremont, MA 01258-0333

www.redchairpress.com

FREE Lesson Plans from Lerner eSource
and at www.redchairpress.com

Publisher's Cataloging-In-Publication Data
(Prepared by The Donohue Group, Inc.)

Names: Prokos, Anna. | Kendall, Gideon, illustrator.
Title: No bones about it! : discovering dinosaurs / by Anna Prokos ; illustrated by Gideon Kendall.

Description: South Egremont, MA : Red Chair Press, [2017] | Imagine that! | Interest age level: 006-009.
   | Includes Fact File data, a glossary and references for additional reading. | Includes bibliographical
   references and index. | Summary: "Have you ever seen an elephant in a zoo? You know they are very
   big and can weigh as much as a school bus! Millions of years ago there was a dinosaur on Earth called
   Brachiosaurus. One Brachiosaurus weighed as much as 17 elephants! Can you imagine how big some
   dinosaurs must have been? In this book, readers explore a world where dinosaurs roam. And learn
   fascinating facts about dinos along the way."-- Provided by publisher.

Identifiers: LCCN 2016934110 | ISBN 978-1-63440-150-0 (library hardcover) | ISBN 978-1-63440-156-2
   (paperback) | ISBN 978-1-63440-162-3 (ebook)

Subjects: LCSH: Dinosaurs--Juvenile literature. CYAC: Dinosaurs.

Classification: LCC QE861.5 .P76 2017 (print) | LCC QE861.5 (ebook) | DDC 567.9--dc23

Technical charts by Joe LeMonnier

Photo credits: Shutterstock, Inc except page 30: Phil Brown / www.sanctuarymountain.co.nz

First Edition by:
Red Chair Press LLC   PO Box 333   South Egremont, MA 01258-0333

Printed in the United States of America
Distributed in the U.S. by Lerner Publisher Services. www.lernerbooks.com

1116 1P CGBS17

Have you ever seen an elephant in a zoo? You know they are very big and can weigh as much as a school bus! Millions of years ago there was a dinosaur on Earth called Brachiosaurus. One Brachiosaurus weighed as much as 17 elephants!

Can you imagine how big some dinosaurs must have been? Are you ready to explore a world where dinosaurs roam?

Table of Contents

"Gather around," the museum guide told the class. "Don't worry, he won't bite!"

Lee and his friends laughed and stepped closer to the Argentinosaurus. The dinosaur towered over the group. Lee had never seen anything as big as this dinosaur before.

Lee stared at the dino's long neck. Its head nearly reached the ceiling! "That must have been the biggest dinosaur ever!" he exclaimed.

6

"It's the biggest dino ever found so far," the museum guide said. "Scientists figure out how big a dino was by looking at **fossils**. To estimate the size of this Argentinosaurus, scientists studied the size of its thigh bone and backbone."

"Where are dino fossils found?" Lee asked.

"Great question! Bones from this dino were found on a farm in Argentina in 2003. But fossils have been found in many places around the world," he said pointing to the map.

8

IT'S A FACT

About 245 million years ago, all Earth's land was joined in one supercontinent (Pangea). Gradually over millions of years, Pangea broke apart and the smaller land masses drifted to their present locations. This may explain why fossils are found everywhere.

Lee took a closer look at the map.
He noticed that many fossils had been
discovered near mountains. But how do
fossils end up on a mountain, he wondered.

Suddenly, a hot, sticky breeze swirled by.
In an instant, Lee was surrounded by
a lush, green forest.

Ferns and bushes covered the ground.
Plants as tall as trees towered over him.
They created shadows on the thick, dirt ground.

"That's strange," Lee said. "This plant's shadow is in the shape of a dinosaur!"

The shadow moved. It got closer and closer. Lee felt the ground tremble.

IT'S A FACT

Prehistoric forests were mostly conifers and huge evergreens.

"That shadow is not from a plant! It belongs to a d-d-d-dinosaur!" Lee couldn't believe his eyes! A group of dinos was heading in his direction.

The herd rambled closer. Bigger dinos led the pack. Smaller ones trailed behind. All of them left deep tracks in the moist soil.

Lee stared at the **prehistoric** creatures. Their skin looked thick and saggy, like an elephant's. Their necks stretched high and long, like a giraffe's. And four hefty legs held up their bulky bodies.

The herd happily plucked leaves from the trees and plants. "Phew!" Lee sighed. "These **herbivores** won't eat me for lunch!"

IT'S A FACT

The crocodile group of dinos included the Protosuchus who lived on land more than modern crocodiles.

Lee explored the ancient world. He wondered why he didn't see many mountains, like on the museum map. But a few things looked familiar.

A dinosaur that looked just like a big bird swooped to the lake to snag a fish. Two other dinos looked like crocodiles—but bigger.

"I think I'll stay away from those **carnivores**!" he said, backing away.

IT'S A FACT

One of the earliest flying dinos, the Archaeopteryx, had a body covered in feathers. A wishbone made its chest stronger for flapping and flying, like today's birds.

Suddenly, a loud roar rang through the forest.
The birds and small animals scattered to hide.
The large herbivores stopped in their tracks.
Even the croc dinos slinked away.

"Wh-Wh-What was that?" Lee trembled.
The roar sounded angry, hungry—and very
close. Could it be a...

IT'S A FACT

One of the most-feared dinos ever was Tyrannosaurus, living 70 million years ago. It was 40 feet long and 20 feet high weighing 7 tons. Its saw-like teeth were 6 inches long, to rip meat apart.

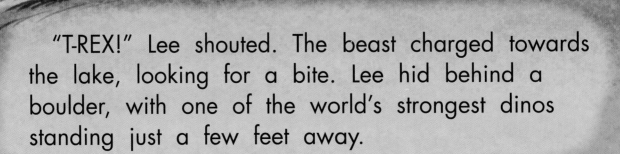

"T-REX!" Lee shouted. The beast charged towards the lake, looking for a bite. Lee hid behind a boulder, with one of the world's strongest dinos standing just a few feet away.

Suddenly, the ground shook. It rumbled
and rocked. Earthquake! Trees collapsed.
Rocks tumbled. No matter how hard it tried,
the mighty dino couldn't escape the disaster.

Minutes later, the forest was silent. Mounds of dirt covered the dino tracks. The lake was half its size. The rest of it was filled up with mud. The creature-filled forest was now eerie and quiet. What happened to the dinosaurs?

Suddenly, a cool, wet breeze blew by. Lee opened his eyes back in the museum. "Earth is like a big layer cake," he heard the guide say.

"The bottom layer is made of older rocks and fossils. Over time, dirt and rocks covered that layer to form a newer one. As more time passed, the Earth changed again. There were big storms and volcanic eruptions."

"And earthquakes!" Lee added with a wink.

"That's right!" the guide said. "Shifts in the Earth's crust cause the land to change over time. What was once the ground can get pushed up to form mountains. That's why dino fossils can be buried deep in the Earth or found high on a mountain."

"And that's why dinosaurs are dynamite," Lee said. "No matter where you find them!"

The Reign of Dinosaurs: Mesozoic Era
245 to 65 million years ago

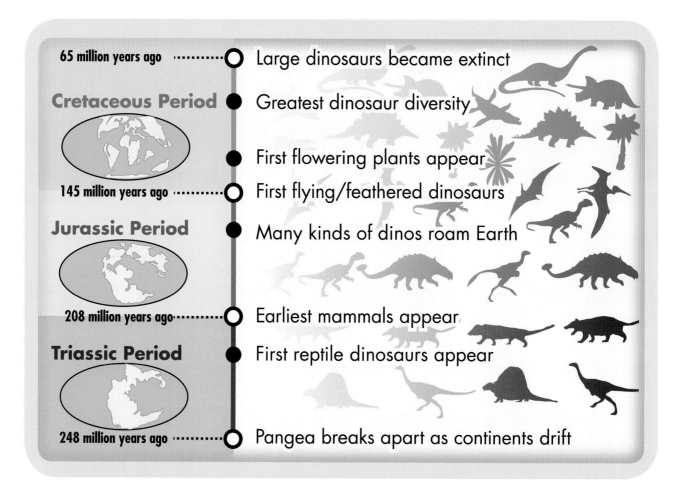

65 million years ago ·········· Large dinosaurs became extinct

Cretaceous Period — Greatest dinosaur diversity

First flowering plants appear

145 million years ago ·········· First flying/feathered dinosaurs

Jurassic Period — Many kinds of dinos roam Earth

208 million years ago ·········· Earliest mammals appear

Triassic Period — First reptile dinosaurs appear

248 million years ago ·········· Pangea breaks apart as continents drift

Scientist do not know exactly why there were mass extinctions of the large dinosaurs. Some believe a large meteor up to 6-miles wide may have struck Earth in today's Central America causing global climate change.

Dinosaurs Around the World

Allosaurus
strange reptile
Age: Late Jurassic, 150 million years ago
Size: 16.5 feet high, 39 feet long
Fossils found: Colorado (USA), Africa, Australia
Note: A cousin of Tyrannosaurus. Walked on its back legs. Carnivore with strong jaws and saw-like teeth.

Gallimimus

chicken mimic
Age: Late Cretaceous, 70 million years ago
Size: 9 feet high, 20 feet long
Fossils found: Mongolia
Note: Features in common with early birds and ostrich. Could run very fast but didn't fly.

Ankylosaur
fused reptile
Age: Late Cretaceous, 70 million years ago
Size: 10 feet high, 33 feet long
Fossils found: North and South America (Bolivia)
Note: Covered in bony plates like armor. Had a huge bony club at the end of its tail for defense. Herbivore.

Iguanodon
iguana-like
Age: Cretaceous, 120 million years ago
Size: 16 feet high, 30 feet long
Fossils found: Europe, North Africa, Asia
Note: Large brain, well-developed senses. One of the first full set of dino fossils found.

Archaeopteryx
ancient wing
Age: Late Jurassic, 150-145 million years ago
Size: Like a large eagle with 18-inch wingspan
Fossils found: Germany
Note: Like modern birds. Covered in feathers, hollow bones, & chest wishbone.

Leaellynasaura
Leaellyn's lizard
Age: Cretaceous, 110 million years ago
Size: 2 feet high, 8 feet long
Fossils found: Australia
Note: Good eyesight helped it see in the dark when Australia was within the southern Polar region before continents drifted apart. A long tail wrapped around its body for warmth.

Pangea

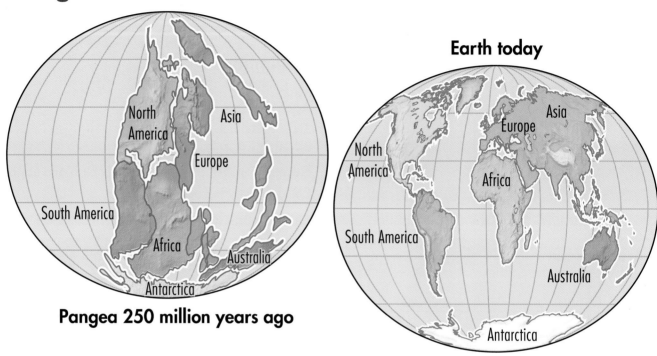

Pangea 250 million years ago

Earth today

At the beginning of the Triassic period the continents were joined together as one huge super continent, called Pangea. Then at the start of the Jurassic period, the land drifted apart as a rift appeared (maybe from a series of earthquakes). This rift became the Atlantic Ocean.

During the later Cretaceous Period, the southern continents split apart and Europe drifted north.

This explains why similar dinosaur fossils are found on different continents now.

Kids Lead the Way!

On a hot summer day in 1999, a 12-year-old boy named Miguel Avelas gave **paleontologists** in Argentina's Patagonia region a big surprise. He led them to a place where they found 90 million-year-old fossils of sharp-beaked reptiles called Sphenodontians.

The only living Sphenodontian descendant is the tuatara, found only in New Zealand.

Scientists had thought the lizard-like reptiles disappeared more than 120 million years ago. "It was fantastic," one of the scientists said. "We had no idea that Sphenodontians could possibly be found there." For Miguel, it was just a playground in the red sandstone cliffs.

Words to Keep

carnivore: an animal that feeds on flesh or the meat of other animals.

fossils: remains of a prehistoric plant or animal preserved as a mold or cast in rock.

herbivore: an animal that feeds on plants.

paleontologist: a scientist who studies fossils of plants and animals.

prehistoric: the time before there were written records of events.

31

Learn More at the Library

Books

DK Kids with Smithsonian Instituition. *Dinosaur!* Dorling Kindersley, 2014.

Ray, Deborah Kogan. *Dinosaur Mountain: Digging Into the Jurassic Age.* Farrar Straus Giroux, 2010.

Walters, Bob and Tess Kissinger. *Discovering Dinosaurs.* Applesauce Press, 2014.

Web Sites

Discovery Kids
http://discoverykids.com/category/dinosaurs/

Index